With thanks to Julissa, Cyrus and Jim
for their love and support.
JE
To Andrea, Lorène, Sonia and Christophe
Thanks for being part of my adventures.
DJ
Special thanks to Niamh Foran for her generous support.

This book would not have been possible without the generous support of

National Bank of Dubai

Published in 2005 by JERBOA BOOKS
P O Box No 333838 Dubai U A E
www.jerboabooks.com
ISBN 9-948-426-25-8
Copyright © Janice Edgar/ Donna Acheson 2005
Printed in India

Pierre's
Adventure in Arabia

Searching for the Heart of Dubai

by Janice Edgar

Illustrations Donna Acheson-Juillet

It was a cool, windy day. The air was crisp and the leaves in the forest were exploding with colour. Pierre was preparing for a long flight.

At the start of every winter, he and his family and friends took to the air. They flew out of Canada to a warmer place.

But this year things were different. Pierre was going to fly alone, without his mum. He wasn't sure where he was going, but he was determined to find a splendid adventure.

Pierre flew for many days. At one point he looked down and all he saw was water. It seemed to go on forever. He was very tired when he finally saw a shoreline in the distance.

His wings tingled with excitement as his feet finally settled on a mound of soft, warm sand. Everywhere he looked there was sand. Sand, sand and more sand.

The sun was hot on his back and the sky above was hazy blue. He saw some pink flamingos standing in a pool of water and flew over to join them. 'I'll land right in the water to cool off,' he thought. What a surprise - even the water was hot.

He flapped his wings to make a breeze. The tip of his wing hit a small butterfly passing by, knocking it into the water. The butterfly coughed and sputtered while Pierre stared at it.

'*As-salaamu alaykum*,' said the butterfly softly while she fluttered shyly in the air.

'Pardon me,' said Pierre, 'I'm sorry.'
The butterfly studied Pierre. He was not like the other birds she saw around.

'*Tatakallam Arabee* - can you speak Arabic?' she asked the strange bird.

'I'm Pierre and *je parle français* but I don't know any Arabic,' he replied. 'Who are you?'

'My name is Faarasha Farhana, in Arabic it means happy butterfly. '*Marhaba* - hello,' she said, giving him a warm smile.

'Where am I, Farhana?' asked Pierre.

'You are in Dubai, which is part of Arabia,'
she said, while drawing a rough map
in the sand to show him.

'Dubai is one of seven
emirates that makes up the
United Arab Emirates. I can
show you around if you like,'
she added.

'I'd like that very much,' said Pierre, 'but first,
I need to rest.'

'*Mafi mushkila* - no problem,' she said.

Farhana led Pierre to a shady area. A warm breeze rustled the acacia leaves gently. They nibbled on dates and sipped coffee poured from a long-necked pot into tiny cups.

After sharing stories about themselves and their families, they rested in the shade. Then Pierre closed his eyes and nestled into the soft comfort of the cushions. He could hear cars in the distance. The familiar sound aroused his curiosity.

'That noise I hear in the distance; is that where the heart of Dubai lies?' asked Pierre.

Pierre's question surprised Farhana. She didn't know what to say. She had lived in Dubai all her life and had never really thought about it.

'Where is the heart of Dubai?' she asked herself.

Was it in the traditional souks or in the modern city buildings? Could it be out in the vast desert or along the shell-strewn beach? Was it among the camels or hiding in a wadi? She didn't know, but now she too wanted to find out.

'I don't know the answer to your question, but I'd be happy to help you find it!' she exclaimed.

Suddenly Pierre heard voices travelling across the sand.
'What's that sound I hear?' asked Pierre.

Farhana looked at Pierre with astonishment.
How could he not know the call to prayer?
It rang out five times a day.

'Why, that's the call to prayer,' she said,
explaining that people from Dubai are
Muslims. Pierre listened quietly as she told
him about Islam and its traditions.

'I'd love to see a mosque,' he said.

They flew in the direction of the voices. Pierre settled on a crescent at the top of the highest dome. Together, they watched the people below remove their shoes before entering the mosque.

As the evening wore on, Pierre's eyes grew heavy and he fell fast asleep. At the crack of dawn, he awoke to the musical call to prayer. He gazed across at the horizon and was delighted to spot Farhana, his new friend, flying over to greet him.

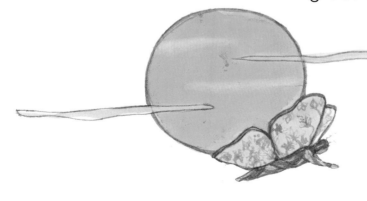

'*Yallah, Yallah* - Come on!' she said excitedly, 'Let's look for the heart of Dubai!'

First they went to a souk where narrow alleys snaked off in many directions. Pierre felt like he had stepped back in time. Merchants beckoned people to come into their little shops. He could hear them haggling over prices.

Many of the people wore traditional clothes. 'The men's gown is called a *dishdasha* and a *ghutra* is worn on the head. The long black gown the women wear is called an *abaya*, and the veil covering the head and face is a *shayla*,' said Farhana.

'Is this the heart of Dubai?' he asked Farhana.

'It might have been here in the past, but I'm not so sure this is where it is now,' she replied.

Next, Farhana suggested they board an *abra*, so that they could look for more clues among the traditional souks and modern buildings on the other side of the Creek.

'People first started trading goods around the Creek, which is where Dubai was born. I think today, however, its heart has been transplanted,' said Farhana.

While puzzling over her comments, Pierre pointed at the odd chimneys. He asked Farhana why anyone would need a fireplace in this hot climate. Pierre's comment delighted Farhana - and she chuckled softly at his confusion.

'Those aren't chimneys, they're *barajeel*. They help keep the buildings cool during the hot summer months,' she said.

The air on the other side of the Creek was filled with sweet aromas. However, they both agreed that although the 'spice souk' had a hearty smell, it wasn't the heart of the city.

'I like to believe Dubai has a heart of gold,' said Farhana as they wandered through the gold souk, 'but I don't think that means its heart is here.'

Pierre agreed. Windows dazzling with gold lined a covered walkway for a long stretch. It was indeed an amazing sight, but it wasn't what they were looking for.

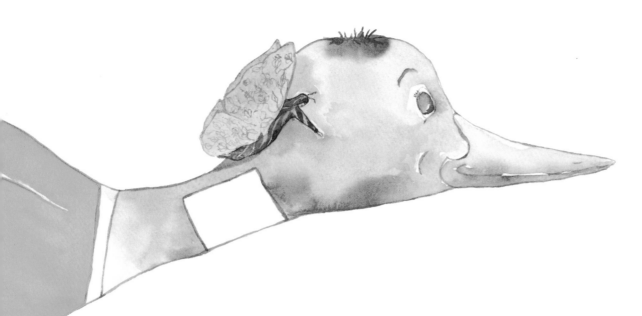

A short distance away, the streets were filled with honking cars. Shiny, tall buildings reached to the sky. Fancy shops lined the streets. The traditional souks were gone.

They darted among the modern structures, searching for clues, but still found no answer.

It was one o'clock. Most of the shops closed for a midday break. Farhana said it would be a good time to go to the beach and rest.

'Perhaps we'll find what we are looking for amidst the roar of the crashing waves, or somewhere along a stretch of soft, hot sand,' she said enthusiastically.

As they lay peacefully under the blazing sun, they watched children scampering among the rocks in the distance. Farhana said they were probably searching for crabs and collecting special treasures from the sea.

As they lazed, admiring the sea, Pierre felt certain they were getting closer to their goal.

Later, they basked in the sun's warmth while floating in the
cool water of a swimming pool. It was like being in an oasis.
They were shaded by tall palm trees and lush plants.

Pierre thought it was heavenly. He gazed up at the
endless stretch of blue sky and wondered
aloud where else the heart of Dubai
could possibly be.

Farhana gazed fondly at her new friend.
She admired his determination and tried to
think of new places they could explore,
to continue their search.

Early the next morning they left the city. Farhana thought they might find some clues in the vast, open desert. They bumped and jostled as they drove across the sand.

Pierre's heart pounded as they neared the top of one of the biggest sand dunes, which offered an amazing view.

'Maybe the heart of Dubai is somewhere out here?' Farhana said, pointing to the endless rolling dunes. Suddenly, they began plunging downwards. Pierre's heart leapt with excitement as he gripped the edge of his seat tightly.

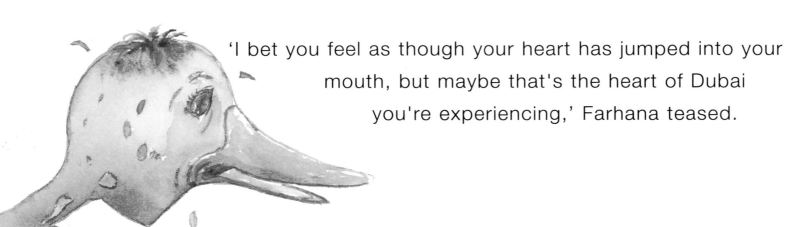

'I bet you feel as though your heart has jumped into your mouth, but maybe that's the heart of Dubai you're experiencing,' Farhana teased.

Later they looked for clues while 'wadi-bashing'. They bounced along a path of rocks as they zigzagged over a gravel riverbed.

'The path we are following is called a *wadi*, a dried up riverbed,' explained Farhana. 'It fills with water and becomes a river when it rains.'

It all seemed so strange to Pierre. He tried to imagine how it would look with water and glanced anxiously upwards. It was reassuring to see a mass of endless blue sky with not a cloud in sight.

As evening fell, they sat quietly next to a campfire and reflected on the day's activities.

Pierre chuckled to himself softly. 'I was just thinking how silly I am - searching for the heart of your world in all those fascinating places. I suppose there is a piece of its heart in all the places we visited but it seems I missed the obvious. I found Dubai's true heart minutes after I arrived. It's in you, Farhana, in you and your people. Sharing this quest with you has helped me truly appreciate your world. *Shukran*.'

Pierre sighed contentedly and smiled warmly at Farhana. He couldn't wait to tell his family and friends back home about his new friend and their wonderful adventure.

Glossary

abra	water taxi
as-salaamu alaykum	general greeting (Peace be upon you)
barajeel	wind towers
mafi mushkila	no problem
marhaba	hello
shukran	thank you
souk	traditional market
tatakallam Arabee?	do you speak Arabic?
Yallah	come on, hurry

je parle français	I speak French

The Canada goose is North America's most common goose. It has a brown body with a black head. Its long black neck has a white chin strap, which is a distinguishing feature.

Canada geese nest from southern Canada up to the high Arctic tundra. They travel long distances in their annual migration and generally migrate in family groups. Although some geese, which live in urban areas, winter in Canada, the majority fly south to the United States and even Mexico.

Originally a North American bird, the Canada goose has also successfully adapted to Britain and Scandinavia.

The United Arab Emirates is a country that borders the Arabian Gulf. It is composed of seven emirates: Abu Dhabi (the capital), Dubai, Sharjah, Ajman, Ras Al Khaimah, Fujairah and Umm Al Quwain. Dubai is the country's commercial and transport hub and a popular tourist destination.

Janice Edgar is a Canadian who moved to Dubai in August 1999 with her husband and two children, then aged five and seven. Their relocation to Dubai represented the family's first international move and introduction to life as expatriates. She is a graduate of Carleton University's School of Journalism (Ottawa, Canada) and is keen to share her enthusiasm for their 'new home' with people everywhere.

Donna Acheson-Juillet was born and raised in Montreal, Canada and spent 12 years in Grenoble, France before moving to Dubai with her husband and three daughters in January 2001. She is an accomplished artist specialising in watercolour and mixed media and exhibits her work and teaches art in France and the United Arab Emirates. This is the second children's book she has illustrated. Her paintings can be found in several galleries in Dubai.

Pierre is a Canada goose who spends most of his time on the shores of Georgian Bay in the province of Ontario, located in central Canada. He generally heads 'south' for the winter but decided to alter his plans one year and landed in Arabia.